To Clever Lily —

clever crow

by Cynthia DeFelice   Illustrated by S.D. Schindler

HAW! HAW! HAW!

♡

Cynthia DeFelice

ATHENEUM BOOKS FOR YOUNG READERS

2005

Atheneum Books for Young Readers

An imprint of Simon & Schuster Children's Publishing Division

1230 Avenue of the Americas

New York, New York 10020

The text of this book is set in Fairfield Bold.

The illustrations are rendered in colored pencil on parchment paper.

Printed in Hong Kong

First Edition

10 9 8 7 6 5 4 3 2 1

Library of Congress Cataloging-in-Publication Data

DeFelice, Cynthia.

Clever crow / Cynthia DeFelice ; illustrated by S. D. Schindler.—1st ed.

p.   cm.

Summary: Angry at Crow for flying off with her mother's keys,
Emma tries to trick the wily bird.

ISBN 0-689-80671-X

[1. Crows—Fiction. 2. Stories in rhyme.]

I. Schindler, S. D., ill. II. Title.

PZ8.3.D3635Cl   1998

[E]—dc21   97-10697

For Bird, of course
—C. D. F.

Clever crow loves shiny things,

Nickels, quarters, diamond rings.

Watchful bird has bright, sharp eyes

on the lookout for a prize.

"Haw! Haw! Haw!"

Swoops right down to take his loot,
Bird he doesn't give a hoot!

Stashes stuff where none can see,
Thinks he's clever as can be.

"Haw! Haw! Haw!"

From his nest old crow can see
House of Emma Wetherby.
Watches from his hidden limb,
Laughs 'cause folks can't fly like him.
"Haw! Haw! Haw!"

One day Mama steps outside,
Chilly! But her coat's inside.
Sets her keyring on the chair,
Back for something else to wear.
"Brrr! Brrr! Brrr!"

Sly black bird spies Mama's keys,

Grabs 'em, flies up to his tree.

Pays no mind to Mama's call,

Pays no mind to her at all.

"Haw! Haw! Haw!"

Emma hears her mama's cry,

Runs outdoors to find out why.

Mama says, "That sassy bird!

He stole my keys, upon my word!

My! My! My!"

Emma looks up in the tree,

There sits bird, bold as can be.

Crow shakes keys as if to say,

"Want to play my game today?

Haw! Haw! Haw!"

Says Emma, "I know what you'll do—
Fly, and hope I'll follow you.
With Mama's keys tight in your beak,
You will hide and I will seek."
"Haw! Haw! Haw!"

Emma thinks, Well, I can't fly.

But no bird's trickier than I.

Crow is smart, but I am smarter—

Gonna teach that bird to barter.

"How? How? How?"

In Emma's room beneath the bed
she keeps a box that's painted red.
Goes to where that box is hid,
Carefully takes off the lid.
"Hmmm . . . hmmm . . . hmmm . . ."

Looks through all her secret stuff—

Gotta call that big bird's bluff!

Smiles when she sees the ball,

Takes it—dashes down the hall.

"Hee-hee-hee!"

Ball it sparkles, shines, and glints,
Smells like Juicy Fruit and mints.
Made of silver wrappers from
Thirty zillion sticks of gum.
"Mmmm-mmm-mmm!"

Emma places ball on ground

Waits nearby, without a sound.

Greedy crow loves shiny things,

Sees that ball and flaps his wings.

"Haw! Haw! Haw!"

Bird he doesn't stop to think,

Grabs that ball quick as a wink!

Keys fall—Emma reaches fast—

Emma's got those keys at last.

"Ha! Ha! Ha!"

Mama says, "Hip, hip, hooray!
I knew Emma'd save the day!"
Key in car and off they go,
Buy some ice cream, see a show!
"Ho! Ho! Ho!"

Old black crow with clear, sharp eye
watches as they call good-bye.
Crafty bird begins to sing,
Clever crow, he knows something.
"Haw! Haw! Haw!"

Soon as folks are out of sight,

Crow comes down from lofty height.

Emma's window's open wide,

Cagey bird flies right inside.

Flap! Flap! Flap!

Lands on Emma's bedside chest,

Looks for treasure he likes best.

Next to Emma's brush and comb

Sees a mirror—takes it home.

"Haw! Haw! Haw!"

Mirror's silver, shiny, small.

But what Crow likes best of all:

When he gazes at his prize,

Sees handsome bird who's just his size.

"Haw! Haw! Haw!"

Now Crow's cheekier than ever,

Got a pal who thinks he's clever.

Mama's car comes round the bend. . . .

Crow's still laughing with his friend:

"Haw! Haw! Haw!"

Mama listens, hears Crow cawing.

Hollers, "Bird, you stop your jawing!"

Emma sighs and says, "You know,

we haven't heard the last of Crow. . . ."

HAW! HAW! HAW!